Maple

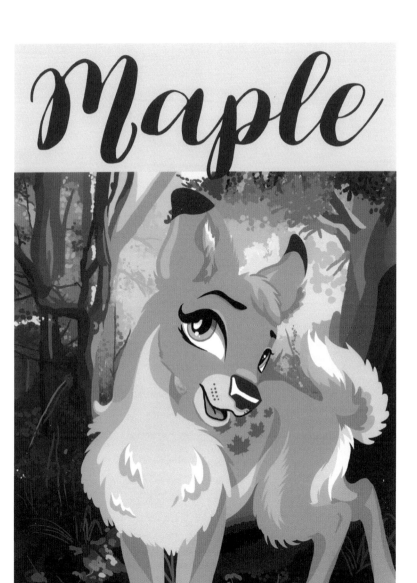

THE MOST FAMOUS REINDEER
YOU NEVER KNEW

BY ERIC J. MUEHLBAUER

FOR FOR BRIANA, ALEXANDER AND CHLOE

ILLUSTRATIONS BY MAGDALENA SYSKA SZLAGA
GRAPHIC DESIGN BY JESSICA VANDER NAALD
EDITED BY KRISTIN GEORGE AND KELLY CAMPBELL

Library of Congress Control Number: 2017914767
c/o Library of Congress
US Programs, Law, and Literature Division
Cataloging in Publication Program
101 Independence Avenue, S.E.
Washington, DC 20540-4283

E & E Media Ltd.,
33 Brook Ln.
Palos Park, IL 60464
USA

www.maplethereindeer.com

The North Pole's Evergreen Forest

Most everyone knows about the eight main reindeer: Dasher, Dancer, Prancer, Vixen, Comet, Cupid, Donder, Blitzen, and the legendary Rudolph with the red nose. But are you familiar with the most famous reindeer in Reindeer Land? Well, her name is Maple and she's probably the most important reindeer ever; but people outside of the North Pole don't know much about her.

This is her story.

Maple, like Rudolph, was born with something that made her different from other reindeer. Rudolph has the famous red nose and Maple, well, she was born with a greenish shade to her coat. She had some dark green spots on her coat too and they were in the shape of maple leaves... so her mom and dad called her Mapledeer (or Maple for short). This made her different from others.

So, like with Rudolph, the rest of the reindeer at first made fun of her. They wouldn't let her play in their reindeer games and sometimes they even laughed at her. But the grown-ups of the herd knew what happened with Rudolph and quickly put a stop to the bullying. They knew that all the reindeer in the herd were important in some way or another. They also knew that the members of the herd needed to depend on one another because they were stronger as a group. If you recall, Rudolph proved his value one foggy Christmas Eve.

Maple showed at a young age that she was very smart. She scored high in elementary school on the SnowCAT tests and was placed with an advanced group. She learned, at a very early age, to use her difference to her advantage. She could hide better than all of the other reindeer because of her green coat. She was very hard to see, so she was very hard to find! In fact, if she stood by some trees and stayed perfectly still, she was completely invisible—impossible to find when playing Hide and Seek. So, she always won!

Also, for some reason, the hooves on her feet were a little softer than other reindeer. So, she didn't make the "clumpity-clump" sound that others made when they walked. It was almost like she was wearing sneakers. Because of this, she could sneak up on the others very quietly during games of Hide and Seek.

Also, because she always ate her vegetables (especially carrots) she was blessed with excellent eyesight. So, she could see incredibly well at night. She could even climb trees

if the branches were low enough and big enough to support a reindeer.

Because of these special skills, she became famous in Reindeer Land. Some reindeer were a little afraid of her – they thought she had magical powers and would say, "No one should be able to hide that well."

You see, Hide and Seek might be a just game to you and me— but for reindeer, it helps them survive in the wilderness. It is especially important to know how to hide if there is a pack of hungry wolves on your trail! Since reindeer aren't very good at fighting, they prefer to run away from enemies—or better yet, hide from them. The reindeer know that if your enemies can't see you, then they won't chase you! So hiding is taught at a very early age and for very good reason!

Her mother, Evadeer, (or Eva for short) told stories of when Maple was very young. She made the mistake of teaching Maple how to play Hide and Seek. Maple learned quickly and loved hiding from her mom. One time, when she was really little, Maple hid from her mom and fell asleep by some maple trees. Maple didn't hear her mom calling her and since her mom couldn't find her, she thought Maple had gotten lost! All the elves were out looking for her. Finally, she woke up and wondered why everyone was so worried about her! Her mother often had to call the elves to come help find Maple. Maple loved to take advantage of her hiding ability when it was time for a bath (which she didn't like) or when it was time to take some medicine. If Maple didn't want to be found, you just couldn't find her!

All of the grown-ups agreed that Maple was quite invisible whenever she was in the forest. Because she always won at Hide and Seek, the most important game in Reindeer Land, there was talk that she might be able to represent the North Pole Reindeer at the International Reindeer Games, when she grew up. (It was very similar to the Olympics, but it was reindeer style!) Representing one's village at the reindeer games was a really high honor.

Herds from all around the world went to the Games. There was a lot to do there. They had a shopping area where you could find great antler polish. The food there was great! You could get fried carrots, and delicious oatmeal with berries, bananas and maple syrup. You could even learn how to weave a basket using bark from a tree.

And the young reindeer weren't left out at the Games! They had an area with reindeer rides. The young reindeer all loved the Sky Slide. It was slide that was as high as a house with three humps in it. You sat on a small blanket at the top and slid down very fast, even got airborne a little when they went over the humps! So much fun! Maple's friends all wanted her to go to the Reindeer Games. They thought she could win the Hide and Seek contest.

Maple's best friend was Chloedeer. They were always together playing. They would pretend they were pulling Santa's sleigh or helping to make toys like an elf. Maple did not get along with Chloe's older brother, Vladideer. Vladideer was often mean to her, calling her "greeny" and pestering her at school recess. He would sometimes come up

behind her and try to kick her back legs out from under her so she would fall on the snow. He was also the only one who could ever find her during Hide and Seek. He must have had good eyes and ears. He was good at hiding too. He was smart. He covered himself with leaves or dirt. He could also be very still when he wanted. He did not like that the grown-ups thought Maple would be best to represent the herd at the reindeer games. He thought he should be the one to do it!

In spite of the fact that Maple was famous, she really was a very normal young reindeer. She liked to play with her friends, play soccer, and she really liked school. When she wasn't playing with Chloe, she could probably be found reading a book.

She enjoyed school, well, most of the time. She didn't like it when Vladideer made things difficult for her. One time, Maple was in a school science fair and she had a good chance to win first prize. She made a really neat display showing how avalanches started and how dangerous they were. Just before the judging, Vladideer "accidentally" bumped into the table and spoiled her project. She still got third place, but she knew her project would have won if it weren't for Vladideer!

Vladideer was a bad reindeer. He was always getting into mischief of the worst kind. He did not like it when others succeeded, so he would do everything he could to prevent them from accomplishing their goals. One day, when everyone was at school preparing for the SnowCAT tests, he pulled the fire alarm to interrupt their studying. He was loud and obnoxious and would often skip class to go smoke cigarettes in the woods.

Once, when the elves were preparing for Christmas and putting the final touches on all the toys, Vladideer snuck into Santa's workshop and poured honey on them. Then, he let in three hungry bears who made a mess of everything by fighting with each other and licking the honey off all the toys. When the elves got to work in the morning, the place was a disaster! It took them three days to get everything back in order and they barely made it in time for Christmas Eve!

Everyone knew it was Vladideer who caused these problems, but no one could prove it. So Santa installed cameras to try to catch him the next time.

As Maple got older, she continued to do well in Hide and Seek games. This made Vladideer mad. He would try to spy on Maple when she hid, so he could tell her opponent where to find her. Maple quickly figured this out and made sure she hid from Vladideer too.

One summer, Maple went to a special "Hide and Seek" school in Switzerland, where she learned the best ways to help her win. She was playing hide and seek a lot because she learned that "practice makes perfect." If she was going to represent the herd at the Games eventually, she wanted to do well.

The International Reindeer Games had lots of different events. There were many running and jumping events. One of these

was the "Evergreen Leap." The winner was the one who could leap over the tallest evergreen without knocking any snow off of it. Another was the "100 Meter Sleigh Dash," where a single reindeer had to pull a sleigh full of toys for 100 meters, going as fast as he or she could. The one with the quickest time won. There was a relay race, called the "Teddy Relay", where one team member would run around the track with a teddy bear in its mouth, giving it to the reindeer in front of them and

seeing who could make it around a track the fastest. Dasher, in particular, was very good at this event.

There was a charity Dance-a-Thon where the reindeer would compete by seeing who could dance the best and the longest. Dancer, of course, always seemed to win this event, though Prancer was always very close. There was also the bark stripping contest. The reindeer who could pull the longest strip of bark from a tree would win that event. Donder was really good at this event, while Blitzen was not far behind. There was a beauty contest. Usually won by Vixen. And a poetry contest usually won by Cupid. There was even an astronomy contest, naturally won by Comet!

To start out the games, they would have Rudolph light up his nose! For the Olympics, fans take turns carrying a torch all the way from Greece to the site of the Olympics. It helps spread the word and build excitement. So the elves made a special Rudolph Red Nose that lit up very brightly and reindeer from different herds would take turns wearing it as they ran from town to town to spread the word about the Games. One time, Vladideer tried to steal it as it went past, just to interfere! But Blitzen, who was wearing it then, was too fast for him and jumped away as Vladideer tried to get it!

6

One of the most popular contests was a game called "Spook." Besides Hide and Seek, it was one of the highlights of the reindeer games. In the game of Spook, five reindeer would gather in a clearing and form a circle. A clearing is a dangerous place for a reindeer because predators can see them, so it made reindeer a little jumpy to be in any open area. Once everything was quiet, some recorded sounds would be played over a loudspeaker. These would mostly be sounds of other animals in the woods. They would play "safe" sounds like a woodpecker pecking on a tree (rat-a-tat, tat, tat, tat); a grumpy bear lumbering through the woods (thump, thump, thump); a caribou leaping over some bushes (farumph, farumph, farumph); some geese flying overhead (honk, honk, honk); or a raccoon looking for food (rustle, rustle, rustle).

But there were also dangerous sounds like a band of howling coyotes (aahoooo!

aahooo!); a pack of hungry wolves (grrr! grrr! grrr!), a hunter walking in the forest (crunch, crunch, crunch), a gang of mean badgers (reer! reer! reer!), the sound of a snow leopard crawling through the evergreens (growl, growl, growl), and a cranky polar bear (thump, thump, thump). All of these are very dangerous sounds for reindeer to hear.

The point of the game was to see who could recognize the sound of danger first and run to the forest before everyone else. Initially, everyone stayed in a circle in the clearing.

Then, a sound would be played. It would be played very softly at first, then a little louder each time. If the sound meant DANGER, the reindeer had to race to the woods! The last one to make it to the woods would be eliminated from the competition. But if the sound played was a safe sound and a reindeer ran out of the circle, they would also be eliminated from the competition. So this game tested a reindeer's hearing ability and ability to understand what danger sounded like. This is another very valuable skill for reindeer to have.

The most popular event was always the Hide and Seek contest. Everyone knew that the winner of this event would get all the attention. They would get to meet Santa and they would win a year's supply of tropical fruit, a very rare treat in the North Pole! The game went like this: the two opponents would take turns trying to find each other in the forest. A stopwatch was used to see how long it took for one reindeer to find the other. Whichever reindeer found their opponent faster would win! The reindeer who was slower was eliminated from the competition.

When Maple turned 15 years old, the elders of the herd asked her to represent them at the International Reindeer Games as a member of the North Pole Reindeer Hide and Seek Team.

Though Dasher was a regular champ in the Sleigh Dash, the North Pole reindeer had never had a Hide and Seek champion before. Most of the Hide and Seek champions came from Sweden, Finland, or Russia. The North Pole herd didn't do as well because it seemed most everyone at the North Pole was too busy preparing for Christmas to train for the Games. However, because Maple had a special talent, everyone thought she just might be able to win. The elders told her she would bring a sense of pride to the herd if she did well.

Everyone wanted her to go, including her mother and her friends. Though she was a little scared of traveling so far from home, the elders convinced her that she could win and would have fun attending the Games.

The time for the Reindeer Games finally arrived and Maple went with the team to Lillehammer, Norway. The Hide and Seek event featured the top reindeer hiders and seekers from all around the world! RSN (*Reindeer Society Network*) was covering the event. All of the major newspapers were there too. The New Snow Times (they gave great weather reports!), *The Gatherers News* (great reports on where to find food), *Animal Sports Illustrated*, and, of course, *The Reindeer Times* (first to tell the story about Rudolph). Even television networks like *ESPN 7* and *Fox & Hound Sports* were there!

A huge crowd gathered on the hills around the designated Hide and Seek valley in Lillehammer. There were experienced hiders and seekers from every known herd of reindeer in the world. They included: the legendary Tolsdeer from Russia; Maodeer from China; Gonzodeer from the South Pole; Svendeer from Finland; and the feared and respected Olledeer from Sweden. Olle had won the last five world championships in a row and had all the endorsement deals.

He had his own fancy sleigh that was pulled by other reindeer. He starred in a music video called "Purple Reindeer," and he had a line of cotton harnesses and antler polish

named just for him. He was regarded as the best of the best and he knew it too. He was a little too proud of himself and almost always rude to everyone. Nobody really liked him but they couldn't do anything about it because he was the best!

Once the tournament started, it quickly became clear that Maple and Olle would meet in the finals. They were each finding other hiders in record time and both were hiding for a long period of time too. Each defeated 10 other reindeer to get to the finals. Maple found Mia of Greenland in 15 minutes. She found of Breezylou of Canada in 18 minutes. In the semifinals, she found Anastasia of Poland in about 20 minutes. But Maple was able to hide longer than all of her opponents, so she made it closer and closer to the finals. The herd at the North Pole was very excited for her and watched all the events on TV. Even Santa took time out to watch!

It was the night before the finals and Maple could not sleep. After all, this was her first championship match ever and she was pretty nervous about it. She wanted to go home, but she knew that wasn't an option. So, she went out for a walk and stopped in front of an iced over pond to watch the stars reflecting off of it. The full moon was bright and the snow sparkled all around. She missed her mother, who had stayed at the North Pole, but she called Maple every night. Out of the corner of her eye she saw another young reindeer sitting, gazing at the stars, and walked toward him. It was another young hider/seeker named Alexi from Alaska. She had actually beaten him in round 4 and she remembered

him because he was genuinely nice to her and wished her well in the rest of the tournament. Most of the others she beat had just stomped away when they were found.

She also thought he was kind of cute. She knew that he was only a couple of years older than her too. As she walked toward him, she suddenly got very shy and didn't know what to say. He recognized her right away.

"Nice night," he said, trying to be friendly. All she could mutter was, "Uh huuuh."

Then, there was an awkward silence.

He tried something else. "Olledeer sure is good, isn't he?"

Again she muttered, "Uh huuh."

He quickly added, "But you're good too—I mean, you're really good at hiding!"

She replied, "Uh huuh," again.

He thought, *Oh brother, she's not very talkative.* He figured he'd try one more time. He asked jokingly, "What's the matter? Did someone **hide** your tongue and you can't talk now?"

Maple tried not to, but she burst out laughing, then relaxed a little bit and started to talk. She told Alexi about how she missed her mother. She admitted that she was a little scared of all the attention and she just wanted to go home.

He just listened and tried to tell her it that it would all be over just a few hours and that she would be okay.

Talking to him helped her to calm down. They talked for a long time and discovered they had many things in common. They both liked to read books about other places and they both liked to do puzzles.

Finally, Maple said, "I'm getting tired now, so I should go get some sleep. Are you going to be at the match tomorrow?"

He said, "of course I will be there!" It made her glad that he was going to be there.

Somehow, it helped her to feel stronger inside. Finally, she went back to her room, climbed into her bed, and fell fast asleep.

The championship round was quite an event. A coin toss decided who would hide first. Olle won the toss and decided to be the first to hide. He was smart. He put all the pressure on Maple, the young reindeer from the North Pole, by making her hide last. But Maple did fairly well and found Olle in 37 minutes. She quietly snuck up on him in the thickest part of the forest. Not many people know this but you can move around when you are hiding. It is especially smart to go hide in a place that was already searched. So, you have to be quiet when you are hiding AND seeking! Now, Maple had to hide for more than 37 minutes and she would win the championship! She knew it was not going to be easy.

When it was time for her to hide, she found a great spot where there was an old maple tree growing right between two thick evergreens. She climbed up on a thick branch near the top of the maple tree and stayed super still. Since she was out a little late the night before she felt like she had a slight cold and was ready to sneeze while she was hiding but she knew she couldn't because that would give her away!

She noticed that Vladideer was in the stands looking through some binoculars for her (so he could tell Olle!). The sun came out and she realized that she could easily see her breath (and if she could see it, then so could Vladideer or Olle)! But, she remembered a trick that Santa had taught her. If you didn't want someone see your breath, you should eat some snow! It makes your breath as cold as the air so it would not be visible.

Maple hid and hid and stayed as still as she could. She almost sneezed once. But she didn't. Olle even walked by her ***three times***

and never saw her. She ate snow as she saw
him approach and she stopped herself from
sneezing! Time seemed to drag on and on!

When will it be 38 minutes?!?!? She wondered. The clock kept ticking: tick tock, tick
tock, tick tock. Olle started to get desperate
and began yelling that there were wolves near-
by to try and frighten Maple. But she didn't
budge. Finally, the clock read 38 minutes!

Maple had won!!! The crowd cheered!
A band started playing and Maple climbed

down from her perch near the top of a maple tree! Everyone congratulated her!

Olle, of course, was very mad. He could not believe it! He lost! And he had been beaten by a young reindeer from the North Pole! That was

the worst thing that could happen to his reputation! He stomped away in a huff! Meanwhile, back in the North Pole, everyone watching on TV celebrated! When they placed the gold medal around her neck the herd was very, very proud of her!

Maple was still kind of shy about the whole thing. She was not comfortable with all the attention. A reporter and photographer from the *Reindeer Times* wanted to do a story about her and put it in the paper. She let them interview her and then they wanted a picture. Maple was very bashful about being in the paper but she agreed. But she tricked them by standing in front of the clump of maple trees. When the photographer got back and developed the film, he could not see a reindeer in the photo! Maple blended in that well! So, he just ran the story without the picture, which is the way Maple wanted it in the first place.

Because she won first place in the Hide and Seek event at the International Reindeer Games, Maple had many endorsement offers from deer shoe manufacturers like, Treebok and Hike. They all wanted her to go places to promote their product but she just wasn't interested. She preferred to be at home with her mom and her friends. She was even offered a wonderful position as a scout for Santa. But she turned that down, too. Her mother understood and let Maple make her own decisions. Maple had already shown her mother that she was very responsible.

What Maple really wanted to do was to was to go to college. Maple's father had died when she was very young. (He was caught in an avalanche). She knew how precious life was and how important it was to be with family. Her mother could not afford to send her to college so Maple didn't think she would be able to go.

However, the elders in the herd put together a fund-raiser and gave her a scholarship for bringing such pride to the herd. She also accepted one endorsement deal from Treebok because they just wanted to name a shoe after her. They called it the "Maple Hider" and it sold very well. She and her mom had enough money now that they could even take a vacation. They decided it would be fun since they had never been on a vacation before.

Maple and her mom had no idea where to go on a vacation. They couldn't go far because they needed to stay where is was chilly. Chloe's mom, Maggiedeer, suggested that they go where all the rich and famous reindeer went—the island of Iceland at a resort in the town of Reykjavik. It was rumored that many rich and famous individuals had homes there. Santa's reindeer went there every year after Christmas Eve and stayed at his Villa on the coast to rest. After all, flying all over the world in one night is a lot of work!

Yes! Reykjavík was the place to go if you were somebody! It was also very beautiful there – the land of snow and ice—was a reindeer's dream. It was also filled with fancy little shops selling fudge, jewelry, and perfume.

There was a very nice resort called the Reykaloa Village Resort. Fancy artwork lined the hallways of the main building and rooms were available at the main building and several cabins on the resort grounds. Reindeer staying in one of the cabins could get to their rooms by sleigh, ice boat, or by simply trekking through the snow. Each cabin had its own fireplace and overlooked the ocean.

Predators were not allowed in Iceland because of the little-known law (1865 Geneva Law), which was signed by all nations and all creatures. It was a simple law and it said,

"All creatures need a place to go and relax, free from predators. Iceland shall be that place."

Most of the predators, it turned out, didn't like Iceland anyway, so it worked out well for everyone. It became a virtual playground for the rich and the fortunate.

The largest population of penguins in the world lived on Iceland. Many moved there because it was easy for them to find jobs—because they look so sophisticated (like they are wearing tuxedos). Plus, they had a knack for being efficient servers and they were always very polite.

Iceland was also a great place for sea otters and seals because they know how to entertain so well. They could balance balls on their noses, make funny noises, clap to music, and dance. Plus, they were very acrobatic—they could slip up and down snowy hills in a very funny fashion. Being natural performers, it was easy for them to find jobs as entertainers.

When Maple and her mother arrived, they noticed many of the richest polar bears and walruses in the lobby of their hotel. They had

seen them on TV or in the papers. They were excited to be in the company of such important folks. Maple even made the mistake of walking into the men's club one evening where she accidentally saw Malcolm Forbeswalrus, Warren Buffalo, and Donald Trumpbear. They were playing cards, drinking brandy, and smoking cigars.

Like other North Pole natives, reindeer rarely left the Arctic Circle and at 65° latitude, the resort town of Reykjavík was the farthest south any reindeer would travel. It was thought that if the reindeer went further south than that, they would not last a day because it would be too hot for them. In Reykjavík, Maple would still have to wear lots of sunblock. They stayed for one week and had a great time, but it finally came time to go back to the herd.

Maple remained the Hide and Seek champion for the next four years. She graduated from high school and was ready for college.

Maple asked her mom if she could go to the Reindeer University in Helsinki, Finland. It was not too far from home. Her mother agreed. So Maple, applied and was offered a scholarship for combined athletic and academic abilities. She was so excited! She wanted to study everything: chemistry, physics, history and law. In her second year, she finally decided to get a degree in Physics. She did well in school and the four years went by fast. As she was working on her final paper her senior year, she made a discovery that eventually led her to become the most famous reindeer in all of Reindeer Land.

Maple had heard about the problem that Santa was having in trying to meet the increasing demands of the children of the world. Because the Christmas magic only lasted for one night, or 24 hours, it was getting harder and harder for Santa to visit all the children around the world who believed in him. He had to get to their houses, get down the chimney (or inside the door), unpack the presents, sample the cookies and milk, and get back up the chimney in only 3 seconds. It was becoming an impossible task! Further, more and more children were learning about Santa. So, the number of children Santa had to see was growing and growing! He either needed more than 24 hours to do his job or he needed to visit fewer children. But the number of children who loved him was actually growing, so the only answer was that he needed more time. But no one had figured out how to give him more hours in the day. It seemed impossible.

One day, in physics class, Maple was learning about the fact that molecules made up all matter (which means that little things make up all the big things we can see). She also learned that if you looked at something really closely, you could see a lot more details. She loved looking at things through a magnifying glass. For instance, if she looked at a piece of raisin toast from a couple feet away, it looked like any ordinary piece of toast. But the closer she looked, the more details she could see. And if she looked at it with a magnifying glass, she could see the specks of cinnamon, the raisins, and even where the butter had melted. She also noticed that the bread wasn't completely solid like it looked – there were little spaces in the bread that she could see. In fact, with some pieces of bread, she could look all the way through them without a magnifying glass.

Finally, Maple got a microscope and looked at the toast, realizing that about 20 percent of the toast was actually air!

Maple was thinking about Santa's problem when an idea struck her. She ran to her room and asked all her friends to give her their alarm clocks. There were basically two kinds of clocks that she collected. First were the old-fashioned kind that had to be wound up and would go *"tick-tock."* The other clocks were all digital clocks or clock radios. The numbers on the digital clocks were green or red. She wondered if there was time within time that she could find for Santa.

She looked at the digital clocks with a magnifying glass when she noticed something. She noticed that each digital number was actually made up of seven very short lines (or bars) that,

when lit, formed a digital number. For example, two bars—lit up, made the number one. The number eight, used all seven of the bars. Because the number one used only two lines, this left five bars unused. And she thought, *"Could these unused bars actually be unused time?"* And if so, could she tap into this time to give Santa some extra time to visit all the children on Christmas Eve?! She felt like she was on to something.

So, Maple developed an idea. Her theory was that the unlit bars could actually be unused time. Finally, she put together a chart and demonstrated that in 10 minutes, there was actually a total of 20 extra minutes' worth of time that was unused. If she could find a way to add this to the time that Santa had then, he would have two extra days to deliver toys instead of just one night!

MAPLE'S DIGITAL CHART

Numeral	Digital Display	Used Parts	Unused Parts
1	1	2	5
2	2	5	2
3	3	5	2
4	4	4	3
5	5	5	2
6	6	6	1
7	7	3	4
8	8	7	0
9	9	6	1
0	0	6	1

28 total lines/bars available on a clock.

After testing her theory, by collecting and lighting up the unlit bars, Maple discovered that there IS leftover time on these digital clocks! All you had to do was gather the bars that were dark and light them up and feed them back into the clock on Santa's Sleigh and he would have all the extra time he needed.

Maple created something called the Digital Time Receptor, or "Scepter" for short. All you had to do was plug it into a digital clock through a USB port and the scepter would gather all the extra unused time bars. The unused bars would be given to Santa when he got to your town and he would use his magic to infuse the bars with a special light that only he could make. Santa had a magic clock on his sleigh which would slow down time all around him and give him his own time zone. However, Santa would need to fill up on local time bars wherever he was. Just like a car needs gas, Santa's Sleigh needed un-used time bars to keep on time. This way, Santa would have enough time to deliver toys all around the world in one night!

Santa would need a new supply of time bars in every town. And because Christmas magic would only work for one night, he had to have a lot of helpers around the world to help him fill up his time tank. Children already know that shopping malls and other places have Santas during the holidays. If it isn't the real Santa, it could be a special Helper Santa. In fact, some of them are called "Maple Certified Santas" and they all have a special role to play on Christmas Eve. During the year, they gather as many unused time bars as they can. Then, when Santa comes to their town, they have to stand at the highest point, (usually a church or office building), and give them to Santa when he arrives. This gives Santa enough extra time in each city so he can deliver toys to all the good little boys and girls around the world.

Sure enough, the plan worked! And ever since a few years ago, Santa has been able to deliver toys to every good little boy and girl in the world!

Maple was so good at solving the first problem that Santa went to her with another problem. Because there were so many boys and girls for the elves to watch, the Naughty and Nice lists were also getting quite large and unmanageable. Santa and the elves were still using paper for everything. And even though he did not know how to use much new technology, Santa asked Maple to help him and the elves get into the digital age.

Maple and her friends grew up with computers and mobile technology, so they knew all about them. It didn't take her long to figure out what the scout elves needed. (Scout elves are the ones who watch you during the year to see whether you are being naughty or nice.) They were each given a smart phone with a special app on it called ElfWatchMe. The scouts enter their kid reports and then it is sent to a special database that Santa keeps. It was called "The Santa's Elf Database of Children's Behavior and Beliefs." The website's address is www.elfwatch. me. Parents can go there to see what reports are in there about their children.

Report subject: Chloe Female Age 5

Very sweet girl who has learned how to share with her friends. Sometimes gets a little cranky when told she can't play video games on Daddy's phone. She loves ballet, swimming and soccer. Sometimes she wants to sleep in her mom and dad's bed when there is a storm. She also likes to blow bubbles on the deck. She is nice to other kids at school, and likes her teachers. She is learning to speak Polish much better.

Belief percentage estimated at 100% yes

Recommendation: Very good presents this year but not so much to spoil her.

For example:

(Results of net search 8/21/2017)
Records found: (14)

Source: Elf Scout: Barnabas J86. Santas Elves 2017
database of children's behavior and beliefs,
© ElfWatch.me

Elf code name: Barnabas J 86   **Latitude:** 92
Hemisphere: Northern   **Longitude:** 182
Country: United States of America   **State:** Illinois
County: Cook   **City:** Palos Park
ZIP Code: 60646   **Subdivision:** Brook Lane
Street: Brook Lane   **Number of houses:** 8
Children of record: 10

Report subject: Briana M   Female   Age 10
Mostly nice, but sometimes argues with her parents
and brother. Calls her brother an "idiot" once in a while.
She stalls when eating her vegetables. Is kind mostly to
everyone, and will let her brother have the dog "Kiska"
at night, even when it's not his turn. Likes to read a lot.
Likes to read *Goosebumps* and *BabySitters Club* books

and collects Beanie Babies. She likes video games, and will share the controller with others. Does very well in school and plays well with almost everyone. Recently got some new glasses.

Belief percentage estimated at 60% yes and 40% no (typical for her age).

Recommendation: Some good presents this year (no coal!)

Elf code name: Barnabas J 86   **Latitude:** 92
Hemisphere: Northern   **Longitude:** 182
Country: United States of America   **State:** Illinois
County: Cook   **City:** Palos Park
ZIP Code: 60646   **Subdivision:** Brook Lane
Street: Brook Lane   **Number of houses:** 8
Children of record: 10

Report subject: Alexander   Male   Age 9
Mostly nice, though he sometimes argues with his parents and sister. He likes to help his friends by pushing them when they are on the swings. He likes to play

video games, especially Mario Kart and Donkey Kong. He will take turns with others so he does share. He likes baseball and soccer but does not like to read much. He likes to run around the neighborhood with his friends and play laser tag. He knows how to draw. He does well in school and plays well with almost everyone.

Belief percentage estimated at 70% yes and 30% no
Recommendation: some good presents this year (no coal!)

Elf code name: Barnabas J 86   **Latitude:** 92
Hemisphere: Northern   **Longitude:** 182
Country: Poland   **State:** Malopolska
County: Malopolska   **City:** Szaflary
ZIP Code: 60646   **Subdivision:** Dunajec
Street: Cztery   **Number of houses:** 13
Children of record: 15

Report subject: Chloe   Female   Age 5
Very sweet girl who has learned how to share with her friends. Sometimes gets a little cranky when told she can't play video games on Daddy's phone. She loves

ballet, swimming and soccer. Sometimes, she wants to sleep in her mom and dad's bed when there is a storm. She also likes to blow bubbles on the deck. She is nice to other kids at school, and likes her teachers. She is learning to speak Polish much better.

Belief percentage estimated at 100% yes
Recommendation: Very good presents this year but not so much to spoil her.

Santa found it very helpful to have these reports so that he could choose the best presents for the kids! He smiled a big smile when Maple and the elves showed him the system. He gave Maple a big hug! So now you know why Maple is the most famous reindeer you never knew.

Maple's next big project is to find a way to keep the scepter safe because she heard that Vladideer was plotting to steal it from Santa to wreck Christmas! But that, however, is a story for another day.

The End